Abo

G000077679

Abdullah Khan was born and raised in London and currently studies architecture at the University of Cambridge. His first writings were his journals, capturing and chronicling his most extraordinary teenage moments. This is his first novel. His friends, family and his location remain his biggest inspirations, while in literature, J.K. Rowling, P.G. Wodehouse, Richard C Morais and Chbosky's *The Perks of being a Wallflower* have influenced his writing. He describes himself as a wild creative, travelling widely and sketching madly. The illustrations are all his own work. In his personal life, he identifies with having a disability, LGBT and BAME, all of which remain issues close to his heart and make an appearance in his work.

He is available on Instagram @aak99xx.

THE FACES

A. A. Khan

THE FACES

Vanguard Press

VANGUARD PAPERBACK

© Copyright 2020
A. A. Khan

A CIP catalogue record for this title is
available from the British Library.

ISBN 978 1 784658 14 4

Vanguard Press is an imprint of
Pegasus Elliot MacKenzie Publishers Ltd.
www.pegasuspublishers.com

First Published in 2020

Vanguard Press
Sheraton House Castle Park
Cambridge England

Printed & Bound in Great Britain

Dedication

For my darling nephew,
Pépinot, and my dear friend,
Elias.

Chapter One
Literally Lost

Two troublesome questions:

1) What if your entire future depended on the strange happenings in one single strange night in another world, another dimension far away?

2) And, do you listen to the little voice in your head that says, "Let's go find trouble?" Yes...?

***

You.

Yes, you.

You know exactly how it feels, don't you? I know you do. You're going through the same things I am. Promise.

Hello, you. I say in my cheerful chirrup. You're probably wondering who I am...

I get nothing back from you. You watch on with a confused look on your face, your eyebrows raised.

What am I? I hear you ask me. I am nothing. Yet I am something. I am there and I watch as things happen inside me. I have little control over them. You see, I am the city. I am Cambridge, where our story is set. These streets are my veins and the colleges are my organs. I have 31. It feels funny to watch all these silly humans go about their day. The river flows like my blood through my core. And my heart is….

Well, you? My lead…?

I'm telling you this story because I can see it happening. I watch as the events unfold. Sit tight, my good sir, my starry lady and all you in between; I'll even tell you how this one ends…

Deep inside the architecture of my belly, Elio Husseini lay on his springy bed, feeling lost. Absolutely lost. Sure, he knew where he was and what his name was and who the prime minister was… oh wait, who is it now? His mind was running around in circles. A constant loop. His dark, tanned skin glinted in the thin shafts of light coming through the gaps in his curtains. His dark, almond eyes scanned the room, searching for his sketchbook. Elio had had an idea and he was desperate to scribble it down.

He got up and planted his cold feet firmly on the even colder carpet, or what was left of it. Sure enough, the familiar four walls of his room at Cambridge University stared back at him, containing him. Protecting him. He smiled to himself, knowing he was safe here. But how long will the butterflies remain? They have places to be, too and one day we'll all wake up to a butterfly-free world. Whatever would we do then? He had an uneasy feeling about himself; he was awake now at a strange time, without knowing why or what had woken him.

He scrunched his brow and thought hard to himself, dazed, trying to work things out. Elio scratched his head and looked at his dark reflection in the floor-length mirror that hung behind his door. A scrawny boy of eighteen stared blankly back at him. A whirlpool of thoughts materialised in the icy glare of the smooth mirror.

Imagine this:

You've been plucked from your old life and plunged into this whole new world, with different people, exciting people and traditions and friends and food and age-old architecture. You'd sure feel the butterfly of excitement raging and fluttering about in the depths of your belly. Sure, it's brilliantly amazing, but for how long?

For eighteen-year-old Elio, gone were the lumpy school dinners, the early morning hours spent sat in a cold chapel, the headmaster droning on, drilling into his very skull. The uniforms were cast off; he was no longer confined to his room at home, no more sneaking out or being interrupted by bothersome brothers or suspicious sisters.

At Cambridge, in my loving arms, Elio Husseini woke up to freedom.

He ate what he liked and dressed how he wanted and slept late or sometimes not at all. Elio partied the nights away, and talked to anyone and everyone — heck sometimes he even talked to parts of me. He felt alive for the first time in a long, long while.

But alas, there were more pressing stories to be told. Like tonight's. And everyone knows all parties soon come to an end. Elio didn't realise that university, with all its fun and freedom, was a scary place. Yes, Elio sat on the edge of his bed, terrified. Sure enough, he had worked hard through school, and though his exams had been tough, he had relished the challenge. But before, there was always someone expecting something from him in the end. There was always a due date, always a helping hand, and a register and everyone was marked in and noticeably present. Yet, in this excitingly strange place, freedom was his worst enemy. Now, he could just bunk chunks off his timetable. There was no morning registration. No uniform checks. No end-of-lesson bells. No blaring emails telling him his homework was due. It was all up to him now. This huge burden had been thrust hard on Elio's shoulders. A at just shy of nineteen, what in the world was Elio meant to do..? When freedom was his liberator but also his captor and no doubt his biggest enemy.

Ah, bollocks, he thought. I've just got to get on with it.

And sure enough, he did.

Elio made sure he stood out.

Parties were now Eliocentric, if he could help it, dancing wildly with anyone who'd have him. He had forged fruitful friendships, including his 'fairy-god-sister', as she liked to style herself: Kitty Celeste. He raced around the old town on his bike, his college mates, misty-dumb-eyed Marco McKenzie included, his flailing hot pink bicycle struggling to keep up. It was all about people for him now. People fascinated him, and there were tonnes of interesting ones, all crammed in me, living, creating, exploring and laughing and learning.

Elio was having too much fun inside me.

But one night, he took it too far, and had almost gotten himself expelled. He remembered it vividly, and still couldn't walk past my left finger on staircase A without thinking of that near-miss of a night. An ordinary dark night, Elios's short attention span had beaten him to boredom. He had grabbed his leather aviator jacket and wrapped it tightly around his lithe frame, not knowing where he was heading. He distinctly remembered he had had a sudden strange craving for white-choc-chip soft-bake cookies...

"Ah, Mainsbury's..." he whispered audibly to himself as he remembered that he had only gotten out of bed to traipse to the "main" Sainsburys. But something had pulled him towards the dimly lit stone corridor in the colleges Old Court and he had climbed the creaky spiralling wooden stairs... and finding himself at a dead end.

There was nothing here.

Nothing except a thin window with its broken clasp hanging limply off the frame. Elio pulled it back and felt a cool rush of night air caress his face. Then something instinctively made him slip through the narrow gap onto the ledge outside, as if the air had sucked him violently into the out; he found himself standing on the roof. The slate tiles were cold against his palms, gripping hard as he lowered himself to sit, admiring the view. Being pressed up hard against the strikingly stunning gothic facade of King's Chapel, he felt his hairs stand on edge. An intimate private audience with such a powerful building with a rich history; he felt lucky. He picked up on all the extraordinary details that adorned the building. It looked like presents piled under a Christmas tree, all higgledy-piggledy but ordered and fun. "Many craftsmen had died constructing this... and yet today it still stands, a gleaming beacon of light and hope, a trophy of the gothic age".... he recalled his lecturer droning on earlier today. This was educational. Yes, he wasn't meant to be up here, but surely it would enhance his knowledge of architecture. He chuckled to himself. Elio had wanted to be an architect since he'd watched Bob the Builder aged seven. And now he had to pinch himself, realising he was studying it at this amazing place, creating new things every day, discovering the world around him. The cold that whispered around my body soon seeped in through Elios jeans to caress his. He noticed how ugly the gargoyles and carvings were. Surely these craftsmen were having a laugh... no one would notice a little joke tucked so high above if it looked as impressive from down below. Two faces, it had. Much like almost every other person he knew. We all have them, deep inside us without even realising. We choose to show which face, and when. He remembered a Beatles' lyric, humming quietly to himself. La la laaa... Lives in a dream... La laaa... something about keeping a face in a jar by the door

Elio moved his head, taking in his surroundings. He noticed a slimy ladder snaking its way to the other side of the pointed roof, and he smiled to himself, hearing his own voice in his very own head, as clear as day in the cold night. He was almost out of my reach, on the surface of my smooth skin. I could feel him crawling along my body; it tickled. For Elio, it felt so surreal, but he was being practical, right? He climbed steadily onto the thin rusty

14

ring ladder. It was just about attached, weakly, to my butter-coloured stonework. He looked over his shoulder, ensuring no one had seen him. And then, suddenly a bright flashlight flooded the roof, bouncing off my tiles and almost blinding him. Someone had spotted him on top of me. I had tried to warn him. You shouldn't go climbing roofs in the first place. The topside of my body wasn't for exploring. Nearly all the humans remained inside me, not wandering carelessly all over my skin. I could feel the panic pulse through Elio's veins, as a bulging vein appeared on his forehead, throbbing. He was almost at the top of the ladder, anticipating that glorious views of my extended skeleton and the rest of town. He had to make a decision, or the neighbouring buildings' porters were sure to send someone chasing after him. In a split second, he clambered the last of the rings and stood tall on the edge of the sloping roof. He paused there a moment, the icy air whipping around his face, and smiled to himself. The climb was worth it. He could see everything. He could make out the familiar buildings, but it was strange seeing them from so high above; the buildings he now called home were like little models. Fitting, he thought. He was an architect after all.

I watched as Elio stood there for a minute. He was on top of the world. And then the bubble burst. He remembered the porters. He hastily made for the only way in and out. The staircase window onto the roof. He stopped short. He knew, at the other side of the door, a porter was waiting for him to crawl back inside. He was trapped. Or at least he thought so. Elio looked around quickly, scanning the small space for a possible way down. He sure as hell wasn't going to scale the side; he was about four floors up. And besides, I wouldn't let him. It would damage my soft skin and organs more than it would damage his tiny body if he fell.

And then he saw it. A faint glimmer from a small window that was ajar. He had no idea whose room it was or whether they were in there, but his heart shoved his mind out of the picture. Elio darted for it. He creaked open the small window a little more and quietly slipped inside. His foot landed on a cluttered table. Every inch was covered in books or sheaves of paper. His muddy boots had stained the desk as he'd lost a footing, beads of sweat appeared on his forehead. The room had a dying fire in the grate and old gilt-framed pictures hung on the yellowing flowery wallpaper. With dreaded realisation, it sunk in.... This room was too nice to be a student's. Top floor in Old Court with a view of the river? Surely not. I smiled to myself knowing where in my cavernous bosom Elio had landed. His back was drenched in sweat. This was a *professor's* room. Or even worse the Master's Lodge, which was basically like breaking into Buckingham Palace, right into Her Maj's chamber. Elio bolted to the door, opening it quietly. What he saw made his heart jump into his throat, and he briefly lost the ability to breathe. This was not the exit, but the door to the professor's bedchamber. The burly silhouette of a sallow-coloured sleeping man was just about visible. The figure turned loudly onto his side, and Elio watched his chest rise and fall like a great moving mountain. Elio jumped back, darting for the door. He tiptoed across the thick honey-coloured carpet and sprinted out and down the creaky stairs, his heart thundering, covered in sweat and mud and guilt. Breathing through his nose, he trudged carefully back across the huge lawn to his own bed. The white choc-chip cookies remained unbought and uneaten, captured in the fortress that was the superstore. I loved that part of my body, I thought, chuckling to myself. It was stuffed with food.

But this wasn't the only adventure Elio Husseini was tangled in.

Tomorrow night was another fresh batch of blasted disasters that would leave both Elio and I changed forever…

Chapter Two
Darkness Delights

Sorry, I've been distracted from telling you the actual story.

"You're distracting enough," I hear *your* soft whisper of a voice reply back. I smirk to myself, take a deep breath through my nose. You're talking to me. As you read this. Well, here we go:

It was common knowledge among the older gents at the even older Cambridge University that the ghosts, spectres and phantoms of Cambridge's finest fellows past and present roamed the streets. This happened each and every night, under cover of darkness. The fellows called this other world FantaBridge — Fantasy Cambridge, if you like, where our story is set, and it begins like this:

The two silhouettes of Dr Benjamin Weston and Mr Alexander Fitzroy — or Old Benji and Dear Al as they had come to be known — stumbled tipsily arm in arm down the narrow, cobbled Trinity Lane. Making for the cleverly concealed gateway of Trinity College, they sang loudly as they walked. The two were renowned academic figures at the university and had been life-long companions, revelling in each other's practical jokes and their shared love of Baroque chamber music. As they approached, a startled three-legged deer leapt down from the carved crest of the college and cantered away. This was the norm in this alternative world. Every night, strange goings-on were witnessed by even stranger characters. The old men wandered through the great arched doorway, nodding at certain bricks as the door swung open for them. They were the *only* living link between the Mere Mortal world and this fantastically real fantasy.

"Ah, what a party 'tis going to be tonight," Al mused, twirling the wispy thins of his barely-there beard. They were eagerly discussing the upcoming party that was to be had tonight, upon this hallowed evening. It was none other than the seven hundredth anniversary of the founding of FantaBridge. A glitzy night, everyone who was anyone had been invited. But tonight, the new younger fellows would be sworn in, protecting and passing on this ancient tradition of the Mere Mortal link.

"Why, of course! I've heard we're getting visits from the other place?!" replied Benji.

"Oxonians..." the other trailed off.

"It'll be a terribly interesting night," continued Al as they walked through Trinity Great Court. The ring Al wore on his fifth finger glinted golden as it caught the moonlight. The engraved symbol shone clear, marking his senior status as mediator between the Mortal Realm and FantaBridge. Meanwhile, at the opposite end of the large court, an owl hooted at the two solitary, statue-like figures who'd just jumped down from their cold stone pedestals.

A blue mist sifted through the air; the hour was upon them and all creatures big and small, gargoyles, statues and stone carvings all sprang up, injected with life. Inside the brick vaulted crypt of the chapel, the stiff figures who had been glued to their plinths, were ready to pounce. They had been bound by both the walls of the college and the fate of the day for too long, and suddenly they stood erect, stretching their limbs and groaning heartily.

"Oh bugger," Eweton cursed, for it was none other than the old statue of Sir Nisaac Eweton, legendary scientist and notable prankster that had come alive.

"Joints always get rather stiff at this time of night."

"Well here's to another night in FantaBridge!" Eweton exclaimed, to a hurrah of voices. He was now joined by a jumble of characters, eager for yet another night of exploring. They all wandered out into the tri-coloured stripy lawn, bouncing towards the Buttery.

Meanwhile outside, the two leaders stood waiting to welcome the throng of people that were expected. The chilly wind I breathed had turned Benjamin's nose as red as a chilli pepper. How much longer would they have to wait? The men were soon becoming pretty restless and started to entertain themselves by exchanging jokes.

"Did you hear about the clown who went into a bathroom…? Al's voice trailed away.

"Most of the guests should be arriving right about now," Benji nodded, just as a babble of sprightly voices announced themselves. The group was eccentrically dressed, made up of notable celebrities including Sir Nisaac, who led the group toward the two old figures standing on the far side of the lawn.

A light breeze was dancing up from the surface of the glassy water as the carp leapt up from the depths of the River Cam. I let out a cool puff of air from my architectured lungs. I smiled as their scales glistened in the pale moonlight. They froze for a fraction of a second, before retreating back through the rippling surface without so much as a splash. They too could sense the strange goings-on of the night, and much more that was about to unfold. They were keen to sniff a glimpse of the show.

The wee hours of the night were home to a whole new world. One where time stopped. You see, although time never really bothered me, I did get new body parts cropping up here and there over time. The northernmost point of the night was where the ability to come alive, where cheating death, was *celebrated*.

While the party milled around Trinity's Great Court, and what a wonderful part they were, not to mention the party they were about to be a part of, the noted scientist Dharles Charwin cut a sombre figure examining the different species of flowers and herbs that lined the striped lawns. Pamuel Seypes, meanwhile, excitedly scribbled away in a thick leather-bound journal that was marked with carvings of ancient symbols and animals, the pages darkened with tight handwriting, anxious not to miss any details of this extraordinary night. The jubilant face of Freven Sty echoed the excitement of the great fountain, which had suddenly started hopping up and down on the spot. All over my body, Life was given to even the most inanimate objects, and real fun was to be had in this extraordinary world. I truly became alive.

"Pipe down, young fellow, you'll wake the others," Sir Isaac said sharply to the jumpy little shape. Truth was, the fountain had been looking forward to this night since forever, as his friends — Eweton's Apples had told him how glorious the party would be and how some people even splashed inside the fountain and took a dip. His first real play with humans would happen today!

"Who are we missing?" the two figureheads shouted, scanning the crowd for their dearest friends.

"Why, Stawkings isn't here," answered a squeaky voice belonging to Talon Turing who studied intensely the different faces surrounding him.

"Of course... naturally... er why the long face old chap? Benji addressed Talon. He replied with an even sterner look and moved away to lean against my ribs. His expression suggested he was looking for a clue, some sort of inspiration for his next big project. Although he was incredibly pleased with *Enigma,* he was hoping to apply his findings to more and more machines. Talon opened his mouth to answer when they were all interrupted by a dim hum. The faint buzz could be heard coming from the direction of the Old Divinity Schools. The crowd looked up, anticipating the imminent arrival of more and more friends, focussing on a small light that shone brilliantly bright.

Meanwhile, high atop the soot-toned tiles of the rooftops of Cambridge, Heathen Stawkings' electric chair zoomed around, growing larger and larger. Earlier that night, he had swooped down from his pedestal like a bird let loose onto the thin winding lane. He had hobbled along my crooked cobblestoned arteries slowly, when suddenly, the unsavoury sound of a slow release of air punctured his ears.

"Blast!" he exclaimed loudly, annoyed at just how inaccessible my body of Cambridge was.

"Well, there's only one solution for this," Stawkings continued muttering to himself as he powered his chair to full speed. He flicked a few knobbles and punched in some buttons. At once, up, up and away he was, speeding along Tennis Court Road aiming for the blue-black night sky, chuckling to himself at his own genius. He was a scientist after all and had a knack for inventing and discovering things — the chair was a device of his own making. My vein-like streets shrank in size, as he rose further from the tiny figures, who he guessed were other Fantabs making their way to the party. He spotted a velvety figure punting with not one but *two* poles downstream towards Trinity. He felt elevated, free and at one with the sharp wind that nipped at his neck.

Down below, meanwhile, the group assembled had now swelled to almost twice its original size, and the choir of voices grew louder and louder. They walked past Eweton's apple tree as the man himself started up:

"The apples only float counter-gravity during the night," he explained.

"Hard job fooling the swarms of tourists," laughed the crowd, as Pamuel drunkenly tried to lasso the moon in a feeble attempt to woo a Bambi-eyed woman.

See, in this other world, everything is reversed. Names. Faces. Everything from Laws of science to laws of human attraction. It's an alternative to the boring every day and I'm ever so glad the architecture of my body is the host.

"Where have the apples gone? There's only a couple left!" said Wobert Ralpole questioningly.

"Ever the politician, aren't we, my friend?" he replied jokingly. "Obviously, the finest have been plucked for tonight's pudding!"

Cheering shouts of 'hurrah' and 'yippee' erupted from the crowd.

The crack of fireworks exploded from the college, officially declaring the party well and truly open, bursting towards full swing. Stawkings electric chair darted carefully for the lawn. He messily avoided landing inside the skittering fountain, just as the night sky was suddenly lit up. It looked as though it was from within the heavens, as tiny particles shimmered individually, dancing to the beat of a smattering of applause from the court below. In the excitement, the crowd failed to notice the small explosion that had come from the general direction of the old chemistry labs.

You see, the fireworks were just a huge welcome distraction for some… evil was also at work tonight. There were parts of my bones that made up places that were used for the most terrible of things. I simply had no control over what went on where…

Chapter Three
Mere Mortals

Elio Husseini awoke with a start. He raised a shaking hand to his forehead and found he was dripping in cold sweat. His throat was dry, and his head still ached from earlier. He lay there completely confused, trying to get a grasp of what had just happened. The day had been oddly tiring; he had taken part in a charity race, running from the outskirts of Girton Village, across town and finishing at Homerton College, in aid of Great Ormond Street Children's Hospital. At last, he felt he had achieved *something,* and all in aid of charity.

So why was he plagued with such a feeling of incredible loss?

It was like his very brain was aching. Although he hadn't won, he had enjoyed himself thoroughly, a well-deserved escape from his intense architecture studies. However, the race had not gone as smoothly as Elio had expected; his calf muscles ached and his bones creaked — god, he was almost as used as I was — and ive been around for about 800 years — ive simply stopped counting and couldn't care less. Elio felt a sharp pull on his left calf, his muscles were crying for a break. He had tripped hard and blacked out for what felt like a very long minute, which cost him a lot; he ended up finishing 42nd. The Runners'

Reception, a jazzy event in the evening, had also taken a terrible turn. Seated in the sumptuous wood-panelled Shirkhill Room in Clare's Old Court, his stomach had disagreed with the blue cheese and red wine they had served. Sometimes, the institution that resides inside of me really is eccentrically obscene. Elio bolted out of one the openings in my face into a nearby bathroom, emptying the contents of his stomach. Humans really do puzzle me sometimes. I watched on as Elio's body shook, each belch of vomit was a fish leaping out of his throat into the toilet bowl, which oddly enough started to look more and more like a fishbowl. His head was spinning, and he felt like he was hallucinating. It was ruddy painful. He had then returned straight to his room in a neat tucked away chamber of some organ of mine at the uppermost floor of Trinity's Angel Court. Elio threw himself on the bed, and passed out within minutes. The next few hours he spent heartily in the depth of his own mind.

For Elio, university, especially a place like Cambridge, was nothing like he'd expected. Everyone here was trying to be too normal and too extraordinary at the same time, when mostly the only extraordinary thing about them was their passion. Every person here, including himself, absolutely lived to learn. It was a very different vibe from his previous "class clown" image that he'd now grown out of. There weren't too many "particularly posh people" and everyone just loved to talk. Though it was mostly about their degrees. Elio soon learned that everyone had worked incredibly hard to make it and now felt they were all equals. It scared him how mature some

31

people were, but he'd found his little group. Everyone was just like him; a world away from his tiny remote Scottish fishing village that he called home. Every day, Elio awoke, unable to believe that he called these magnificent buildings his home. Yes, sometimes he felt like a fraud, like he wasn't cut out for such glamour, but he repeated to himself the small mantra his mother had taught him before she died; "if you want anything so badly, work for it and it shall be yours". A tear welled up in his eyes. It had been four years. And while his dad had tried to do everything to make sure Elio had absolutely everything, they were as poor as mice. So coming here, to Cambridge university on a full scholarship meant everything in the whole world. And it made his dad proud, he hoped, and one day, he could repay him for everything.

And now Elio was up before daybreak.

It was like being awakened from a blissful dream, and not being able to remember what it was exactly, but having that shiny feeling all about you. Until even that fades away.

He lifted his legs off the bed, and they felt very heavy. With a jolt, he realised he had slept in his stiff blazer, too unwell to change into his PJs, let alone draw the curtains. A sharp ray of streetlight danced across the ceiling. He reached his clammy hands up to pull the curtains shut.

And that's when something strange happened.

Out of the corner of his eye, he could've sworn he saw the distinctly singular lamppost *jump*.

He shook his head hard and rubbed his eyes. Then slowly opening them, he peered through his heavy lids.

His jaw dropped and he gulped hard, his throat going despondently dry.

There, smack bang in the middle of the cobbled street, walked two pearly white marble lions. The streetlamp seemed to be bowing down to them, a painted face scrunched into a grin on where the glass was meant to be on *ordinary* lampposts. Elio focussed his eyes, hardly believing what he was witnessing. The lions were leading two shadowy figures, dressed in rather eccentric old-fashioned costumes. They seemed to be bickering loudly and Elio realised this is what had woken him. Strangest of all, behind them, a menagerie of miniature figures of animals, statues, figurines and such followed in their wake.

He glanced at his watch.

12:11 it blinked back at him.

What in the world was going on? thought Elio, his eyes bulging.

"What to do, though?" a small voice questioned in his head. His mind was racing, and his heart beat loudly in his chest. Tempting though it was to slip back into the warmth of his bed, the little voice crept up again.

"We could go exploring." It smirked with a cheery grin.

He had to make a decision. And quick. The funny-looking men and the lions were walking away and soon he would lose track of them. Stone lions going for a walkabout in the middle of the night? Was this some party trick? We're those two men simply coming back from a fancy dress party?

A momentary hiccup interrupted him.

His body screamed for him to rest but he shut it down instantly. He was never going to get an opportunity like this, bizarre as the day had been. He hastily wrapped his favourite stripy scarf around his neck, stuffed his feet inside his leather boots and sprinted down the stairs, taking two at a time. He made for the vaulted archway at the far end of Angel Court. He leapt back in delight as he reached it, as a pair of white eyes blinked widely back at him from inside the stone.

No.

It *was* the stone. The building was *alive!* Elio stood there for a long minute, moving closer to examine the bricks.

Then the faces began.

He first thought he glimpsed a pair of eyes winking devilishly at him. This was followed by the holes in the stones which seemed like gaping, yawning mouths. But when Elio turned around to confront them, the thing vanished, only to take up another spot in the corner of his eye. It was maddening. He quickened his walk, telling himself to stop imagining things, or he'd end up in a worse hole himself. Then, suddenly, the whole court was awash with faces, in every nook and cranny. Every crevice, crack and boulder gleamed with a pair of glazed shiny eyes. Fireworks burst overhead and showered him in a glittery light, lighting up the whole world. Rainbows exploded end to end in the moonlit sky with no end in sight, and Elio's eyes were a riot of colour.

What the hell was all this? What was going? It wasn't May Week till next year — that's when all the balls and parties and celebrations happened…

Elio felt a shock of something pierce his entire body. He felt alive, elevated above the court, and for the first time that strange night, Elio felt he could see clearly, hear everything, and he jumped in the air for excitement. What in the world was happening to him?

Then the music began; very faint and shrill at first but getting progressively louder as he approached the gaping doorway to the great hall. It pulled him towards something, he didn't quite know what.

"No! I'm meant to be finding out about those lions" he told himself. It only hit him now that these were actual lions and he was a thin boy and they would probably eat him alive.

"Stop being silly," it's all in your head. Elio had this conversation back and forth in his head a couple of times.

Then, he heard a deep, throaty voice crack the air like a whip.

"Where do you think you're going, boy?" the booming voice of Dr Benjamin Weston demanded. Everything stopped for a minute. The dying embers of the fireworks drifted away.

He stopped dead in his tracks and made his way across the lawn towards the summoning man.

"Golly! Look here, Benji, its Elio himself," the shocked man exclaimed as the light lit up the boy's face in full view.

And then the strangest quickfire conversation took place with the two elderly men taking it in turns to explain, and it went something or other, like this:

"Why, yes, yes, it is!"

"Funny we should bump into you."

"We've so much to explain."

"Why so baffled?"

"Well, you see… umm. Welcome to FantaBridge, Elio, delighted to finally make your acquaintance."

At this point, Old Benji and Dear Al stuck out their hands, grasping Elio's with crushing force. Elio continued to look as dazed as he felt.

"FantaBridge is home to the weird and wonderful figures of Cambridge's finest fellows of the past."

"Yes, dear boy, you'll soon be acquainted with the likes of Sir Nisaac Eweton and Old Heathen Stawkings himself."

"Tonight's the night that dear old folk like us put their feet up and pass on the baton to the younger fellows, as it were."

Al held out his hand again, introducing himself. Yes, Elio knew him as the Master of Trinity and most students knew of him too, but that still didn't explain so much.

"And, yes, we are sadly the last living walking and talking links left to this other world." I guess he really wasn't all that aware of me. My body played host to both FantaBridge *and* The Mere Mortal Realm. And I'd like to think I was very much alive. I'm talking to you aren't i? see I'm not just in your head… I'm telling you this story. And you believe me. I know you do.

"So I'm… dead?" Elio croaked, his voice shaking. He had never been this scared since his old headmaster had called his father in for doing something stupid at school.

"Don't be silly, you're as alive as a raspberry- and they reproduce like crazy…" Al winked.

"Don't worry, we're completely normal, just like yourself" continued Al.

"So, it's time the younger chaps became the central link between the mere mortal and FantaBridge. Tonight, you've been summoned for the swearing-in ceremony. It's all official but should be jolly good fun."

"Now, do come along into the great hall and meet the other lads."

Still, Elio could not find enough words to string together even a small sentence. He just stood there; brow furrowed. He swallowed hard, blinked a couple of times, then felt Benji's hand take him firmly and lead him into the hall.

"Shall we go in and fetch a seat?"

He followed the fellows down a winding stone stairway, and they came into a brightly lit room. It was adorned with thick purple velvet on the walls, on which hung large gilt-edged paintings. It smelled musty, as Elio examined the room, making note of the strange carvings on one of the thick stone walls. It was a small and inconveniently placed room within me and therefore was not used much. Apart from occasions like this, maybe, whatever *this* was.

And then a sinking feeling dawned on him.

He hoped he was not in trouble; it's not often that you get summoned to a strange room by the master of your college, whilst being caught out of bed in the dead of night. He had momentarily forgotten all about the strange scenes outside his window, as the night was now beginning to take an even stranger turn. He was promptly introduced to the other boys who had been given this 'great honour'. The quartet with Elio now was made up of Max Christies, an older, dark-haired boy with impossibly broad shoulders, Peter Pepin, a thin choir boy with round glasses and long floppy hair and a sprightly ginger fellow, Billy Nemes. The boys glanced shyly at each other, sniggering a little, nodding and firmly shaking hands. Elio's gaze met sharply with theirs. Soon the ice broke and all sense of nervousness had melted into nothing.

"Joining you boys are our two new recruits; Elio Husseini and Rowena Williamson." The boys looked around, puzzled, for they hadn't noticed the only girl. As she stepped out from the shadows, they noticed she had an air of sureness about her. She wasn't just another tick in the diversity box — she was going to own her new role. She was here to kick some butt. The boys stared at her as she cemented her sudden appearance. Crowning her head was a shocking sprite of tight curls that tumbled down onto her blushing rose-red doll-like face. She flashed them a toothy smile, and as Max met her piercing gaze, his face flushed red and a tiny row of sweat beads glinted above his lip. He said something that sounded vaguely like a cross between 'hi', 'hello' and 'alright'.

Soon things started to make a little sense, but Elio still felt slightly surprised. The others were older than him and seemed to know what they were doing and Elio had a sneaky suspicion they had been briefed on all this before. They mulled around in my cosy heart, my muscles sheltering them, and as Elio paced the room, he noticed a small cloud of dust rose every time he stepped on corners of the thick rug. Coming up to Cambridge at first, he had felt belittled by the dominating giants of the architecture of my expansive body that ruled the town. My grand building-like body parts were so daunting to little Elio that at first, he got the shivers every time he walked past them. But by now, he had come to love them and know them as his home. In fact, he had never felt more at home than he did at uni. And now he had four extra friends. Soon, he was absorbed in conversation; it was an awful lot to take in and he felt light-headed. They'd moved on from the standard cringey 'college/course?' questions and found themselves bound by their new roles. The group exchanged stories, sipped on drinks and, soon, everyone forgot just how odd things were. One thing led to another and then to something even more. In the midst of all this, the new, younger fellows were made to sign secret books, say solemn oaths and meet more important people. The first time Elio Husseini shook hands with Sir Nisaac Eweton (Nisaac was a progressive shaker-hander and loved nothing more than to do this several times to multiple people — he managed Elio about five time. That, or his memory was shockingly weak) he would never forget. Eweton's hands were ice cold and he got a bolt of electricity dance around his palm and vanish. Maybe Eweton was just a prankster. It all happened so fast and it was a bit of a bore, too much of a whirlwind to really go into. Elio distinctly remembered hearing a vague explosion that had come from the general direction of the science laboratories and his mind wandered back to the scene he had seen earlier. He looked out the stained-glass window and a single star blinked at him, then disappeared entirely.

It was going to be a long night.

Chapter Four
Poisoned Plots

The small vial exploded loudly in a shower of glass and colourful powder, and splattered the pristine white marble tops of my shoulder, that doubled as the chemistry lab for the humans, with a gruesome sticky substance.

"Blasted bats' ears!" a thin wispy voice squealed.

It belonged to a stout man, with thin greying hair. A scientist turned rogue: Catson James. His partner in crime loomed over his shoulders, the much taller and thinner figure of Professor Francis Wick, or just 'Wick' as he was known.

"What went wrong now?" he enquired softly.

"Just… a teeny weeny… upset?" Catson stammered back.

"We've been working on the *Apple Crumble Formula* for months now! We're so close. Concentrate, Catson, come on." His voice broke trying to control the anger building up inside him.

Professor Wick and Catson, the two notorious scientists, had been working on their so-called apple crumble formula for some time now. Having met over a lifetime ago, the two had grown close and quaffed up numerous scientific discoveries including the discovery of the very building blocks of human life: DNA. Yet, they both felt their shining glory was somewhat snatched away. They had now turned to darker means. FantaBridge had offered them a safe haven to work together, even after the very timely death of the professor. But these snatched moments every night weren't enough to continue their creative flow. Time was of the essence. It was simply too short. Hiding in secret every night, not being able to shout about their discoveries and command respect for their projects left a short fuse, and the two had hatched a plan to change the world forever.

Reverse time itself.

But none of that silly time-travelling nonsense you'd come across in films, but a reversal of power itself. I hear you ask — why are you letting these vile men inhabit your body? You see, you're right, I let the two men concoct the plot and go about their evil work.it really wasn't my place to say anything and besides, I couldn't stop them unless I hurt my own body. What was I to do? Sacrifice my left shoulder? Pierce a vein to flood the room they're in? Trap them in by breaking a finger? No, I was simply looking out for myself. I remember 1940- the humans... they damaged my body and it really bloody hurt, OK? Cut me some slack.

Their world, this alternative, magical, bubbly place had been imprisoned for far too long. The Fantabs had been suppressed enough. The more the professor thought about it the surer he was their plan was perfect. Wick had laboured over it precisely and enlisting the help of his dear friend Catson had been most wise.

It was Catson who had suggested the use of their most perfect key ingredient: The Eweton Apple. The date picked for the plan coincided perfectly with both the 700th anniversary *and* the bi-quarterly lunar eclipse. This meant that *this* particular night gave them a whole extra hour under cover of darkness. They had spent months gathering juicy facts and figures about what was to happen in this historic celebration. Then, they had managed to perfect the formula that would enable change and conceal it in the perfect hiding place. The party, they had got wind of, was to feature the most disgusting extravagance. Reverse soundless fireworks, fizzling icy bottomless champagne vessels that never melted and kept on refilling itself. and entertainment from the likes of Jelton Ohn was all just the tip of the iceberg...But most importantly, the gathering was to feature a luxurious apple crumble, crafted from the finest apples found in none other than Eweton's very own apple tree that grew tall and wide in the heart of Angel Court, Trinity College. These apples were the most delightful of treats, crisp and yet surprisingly sweet, with a sharp citrusy undertone. But most importantly, they contained the perfect number of atoms and the exact molecular structure needed to react evenly and perfectly with the formula they had created. And it was to be served drowning in thick creamy Clare custard, a perfect substance to mask the acidic tang of the secret formula. The elixir would give the fellows prolonged life, and would render sunlight useless- usually if by dawn the fellows weren't back on their pedestals, when the first light hits them, they turn to stone.

Wick and Catson had wasted no time in bribing the measly low-earning cook who had been tasked with creating the crumble, by offering him a meaty *steak*, not a 'share' *stake* as the cook had insisted, in this new world.

"How awfully clever of you to *pun*ish him like that — no *pun* intended," cackled Catson.

"I hope our plan comes to perfect *fruit*ion," replied Wick, nodding at the apples with a cheeky grin.

The two together made a most unsavoury, sour pair, who wanted nothing but power, glory and fame, masking their evil doings falsely in the name of science. Ever since Wick had failed to gain a place at Cambridge aged eighteen, he had resented the power in this place. In fact, he hated my body, yet it was what he called home. What a strange man, my body was beautiful. He had blamed the war, and was determined to give it a shot after everything had died down. Not being a quitter, he had applied again, this time with success. Wick never gave up and most certainly never stopped until he got exactly what he was after.

And that was the exact recipe to make a brilliant but villainous mad scientist.

Why had he turned to dark matters, I hear you wonder? Well, when a stray WWII bomb had destroyed his work in the old laboratory during the Battle of Britain, he had to start from scratch. All his precious findings lost. He had worked for hours on end, ensuring every experiment was just right. He was meticulous and he cared deeply about his work, something he found Cambridge championed. but rebuilding something you've already done takes such resilience. The work here was tedious, and he grew feverishly frustrated, channelling his anger into this newfound plan.

The both of them stood there, leaning against my tense tissue, reminiscing over days-gone-by. Ever since delightedly discovering DNA in the dingy wooden backroom of the Eagle & Child pub, bursting into the patrons' lunch to announce that they had "*discovered the secret of life*" Wick and Catson had grown bored of their day-to-day work. Subsequently, they had hatched a plot to reach greater heights. And now, with just under an hour to go before the feast began, it was a race against time to put the finishing touches on the pudding and perfect their plan. Wick scratched his head furiously —

"We never did get the credit we deserved for such a great scientific discovery," he said, sulking into his cup of tea.

"Why, yes, my good man. The mere mortals never gave us respect. We're not praised like Stawkings or Eweton. They don't teach little children about *us,* do they?" his companion added.

"Well, not for long, partner," Wick smirked.

Watching them all this time was a solitary 'ghost' who sometimes haunted the old labs. They sat chattering away to Kasper, whom they had befriended and oh, most useful did he prove! Contrary to popular opinion, he was not a ghost but merely a trapped soul who hadn't returned to his pedestal in time at the end of a night in FantaBridge. A twice-ghost you could almost say. His flowing yellow locks had turned crystal clear as the age had passed him by. He too, like Wick and Catson, had grown increasingly bored of his banal life. unable to participate fully in FantaBridge and not really allowed to live as a man, he had welcomed the two evil genius' advancements.

He had granted them special access to the wine cellar underneath the Old Cavendish Laboratory, which still held remnants of acids and alkalines past and present, all the ingredients needed to create the formula. Everything seemed too good to be true, it was all in perfect position. It was easy as pie!

The Eagle & Child — frequented by Kasper in his days at Catz College, and now — was a shabby timber building that had begun as a coaching inn. You could still hear, in the lonely hours after closing time, the clatter of hooves on stone and the whinnying of worn out horses. With beer for three gallons a penny. It had been the drunken second home to both characters who had revelled in its dark wooden beams who they never passed without receiving a cheeky wink- or a stern nod by from the older beams. Eventually, they had gotten bored of their newfound stardom which hadn't lasted quite as long as they'd hoped.

And *The Apple Crumble Plan* had hatched.

Catson didn't blame his partner, who was always more daring than himself. Poor Wick had been working on a project that measured the viscosity of water at high temperatures. Imagine that?!

"The dullest problem imaginable!" Wick had branded this, pushing away his equipment. The look returned by

Catson had assured him his new venture would be worth his while.

And that's the stuff villains are made of... Geniuses, with years of resentment built tight like a prison, inside them.

Now, everything was perfected. Every drop had been inserted into the apples, which were now with the measly cook. The last part of the plan was to commence tonight.

"Do let's go greet the lions," Catson added, making a jump for his red-velvet tailcoat and matching hat.

The duo had won over the support of the mighty Fitzwilliam lions who could usually be found guarding the priceless art collection in my grand white heart... Every day and every night, the two stood watch and had been doing for the past two-hundred-and-three years. They were loyal, these lions that roamed my arteries and guarded the treasures of my heart, but had grown immensely bored of the banal routine. So, when two mad scientists had shown up with an exciting adventure, the lions literally leapt at the chance. The grasp of the two formidable figures had gone further; some of the delicately painted characters from the art and sculpture collection had overheard the lions' growls and had wanted in. They too felt imprisoned by their golden frames, trapped in this tomb of history and tradition. Now, Wick and Catson had a whole army of 'bad art' behind them.

And on this particular night, the Fitzwilliam Museum was awash with activity. My gleaming white heart-building rose like a mirage, set apart from the honey-coloured stone of the rest of my body. Now, from flower girls to Greek goddesses, the characters inhabiting this colossal castle were restless. None were allowed to stretch their limbs, having to hold stiff poses all day and their flaky skin cast in harsh light was torture indeed. What infuriated them most was the people who came and gawped at them — coachloads of tourists, touching, imposing, trampling into their home and judging and sneering and looking at them with such scrutiny that it became unbearable.

The growing army was now made up of masked mummies from the Near East galleries, winged angels with towering axes, Gods with bull-heads, silvery-white roman sculptures of an antique age and a giant seated Buddha from the basement. My great heart was awash with activity tonight; headless horsemen and twisted torsos roared outwards, Greek goddesses with billowing garments swishing behind them encouraged delicate rosy-cheeked china dolls. Heads of busts, statues and ruins of stone men with missing limbs scrambled up weapons. Butt-naked men with rippling muscles climbed out from their frames, reaching for impressionist ladies with long lithe limbs. Strange veiled women left their shadowy quarters, joining midget men with meringue-like turbans and kingly kings. A great din and buzz followed. The glass cases that were filled with jewel-encrusted pistols, sparkling spears and sharp swords now lay shattered, while the army marched outwards, clutching their tools.

A change was in the air tonight as the two lions padded down onto Trumpington Street and thundered their way towards Trinity, the two formidable figures of Wick and Catson leading in front.

A revolutionary war was on the brink in FantaBridge. A battle to liberate, to set the score straight. And it was all happening tonight, right here, inside me. I was tingling with excitement.

Chapter Five
Party Passions

The great hall was stuffed with characters, ranging from the springy young to the frail and grey, all chattering away animatedly. The familiar figure of Attenborough of the Davids strolled in, casually seated on a sparkly stag, and following in his wake, a menagerie of various *animals*. It was a very different world now, under cover of darkness in my glowing chamber-breast. Many more different characters of note added to the growing throng of life now assembled in the great hall. The Duke of Butterworthy yawned into conversation with the Prince of Walesmouth, who was seated by the great poet Lord Byron. Then there was, seated on the high table, the snappy Eliza Yammond, arguing with Zeera Klaus, both notably notorious female writers. Wirginia Volf appeared with a faint popping sound and made up their trinity, the three witches cackling continuously. Here and there were dotted the few animals who had secured an invite. Pearly white stags with soaring antlers, tiny furry balls of squirrels seated on the shoulders of shining academics and brilliant birds which swooped down onto the piles of food that towered atop the long tables. The candlelight shimmered off the cut crystal glasses, and the clink of cutlery echoed off my old oak ribs. The air was electric with excitement, the chickens clucked in merriment, fuelled on by neighs and hoots, all blissfully unaware of the bitter scene unfolding in the crypt below.

Elio and the others were led into the great hall, just as the party was getting into full swing. There was a great jostling of noise as everyone scrambled to the feet as the fellows processed down the aisle. The new, freshly sworn-in guardians of FantaBridge perplexedly took in everything around them, familiarising themselves with each other and their new world. Elio was shown a seat on the high table. He had never felt so hot under the colour — the whole hall had stood up for him, for goodness sake!? He was usually the one who did the hurried-dropping-everything-to-stand-up-for-the-inconsiderate-fellows.

At first, he found all these traditions and old nonsense funny. But by five months into his university career, he grew accustomed to all the silly traditions. It was his unique little slice of a university experience. Elio's face glowed brighter than a cherry red, though he noticed he wasn't the only one. The other guardians looked as though they were desperately trying to contain a fit of giggles. He was seated opposite his fellow newbies, but next to a vivacious looking woman with a strict dark fringe and Bambi-brown buttery eyes. She raged on about her obsession with tea and how she now had a vast collection with over sixty different varieties. He later found out this was the late celebrated novelist Shary Melley. She had a discerningly Frankestinian look about her. Elios eyes drifted over to the other boys, as the over-the-top-ly confident Christies chortled with laughter, egged on by a winking Rowena, who tossed her head back as she joined

Max, letting out a great guffaw. They, everyone and the evening, were becoming more and more *normal*, but Elio had the uneasy feeling of being watched, feeling a little bit of an outsider. The others were older than him and they seemed to know more. They had been told of tonight's ceremony well in advance and had time to mull things over, let the initial shock sink in and subsequently fade away. It had just been thrust on Elio all of a sudden, without warning. They all got the black-tie dress code right; Elio didn't even know what black tie was let alone owning any. he thought it was literally a black tie or something you wore to funerals that He sat there, a little content to be standing out, even if it was in his striped navy-and-white jumper and mulled-wine-coloured cords. It had all just been thrust on Elio all of a sudden, without warning. All of a sudden, something came back to him. Just like that, he distinctly remembered seeing the boy, who had introduced himself as Billy in his thick European accent, *somewhere*.

Before tonight.

He racked his brains, going over the strange events of the day, retracing his footsteps in his mind's eye.

"I helped you up ven you fainted," Billy responded.

"Um... wha... how?" Elio spluttered, turning ruby red.

"You vere staring at me wery questioningly." Billy grinned.

And then he remembered it. Billy had helped him up and had given him some sickly sweet sticky liquid in a hipflask, claiming it was medicinal and would help him feel better. It hadn't.

"They alvays give me zat job, handing the new recruits the concoction. Im ze oldest of the new fellows. They made us all drink that nasty stuff. Helps you see clearer. *Really* see, if you know vot I mean." He winked.

"You mean you see the faces too?" Elio looked relieved, and the colour rushed back into his face as Billy nodded.

"And the colours, lights and sounds too…" he added.

"just ask the others…" and now they were all immersed in thrilling tales of what each of them could see, desperately trying to outdo each other in just how bizarrely magnificent their descriptions were. I loved the way they talked of my tender tendons and silky skin…

The great orchestra roared into a crescendo, as everybody helped themselves heartily to thick cuts of roast lamb, which they drowned in gin-shot gravy. Fluffy roast potatoes as big as Easter eggs swimming in goose fat were loaded onto plates, complimented by brightly boiled vegetables. Glasses clinked, with shouts of 'cheers' and 'chin-chin' echoing off my wood-panelled walls.

In the middle of all this, Prime Minister Churchill was frankly rather angry. He had arrived late, missing the introduction of the new guardians. His red face glowed in the candlelight and he was out of breath from his long walk all the way from *Churchill College*. Yes, they had actually given him a room in that brutal , cold and grey keep.

Yes, that was the only location of a a Churchill bust, but surely that didn't matter. The statesman's full body was required and that, made the trip all the way from parliament square in London. Did Old Fitzroy think this was some kind of joke? Having someone like *me* live in my nasty namesake, knowing just how far up that dreaded hill and how out-of-town it was. He puffed on his cigar, and a cloud of smoke constantly followed him up the hall as he limped his way through a gaggle of geese to take his seat at the top table. Seated, he loaded his plate with everything he could get his hands on. His plate groaned under the weight of all the food, as he tucked in without anyone batting an eyelid, too scared of an angry remark. On his left, Dharles Charwin struck a match with his paws and blew into a pipe. Ash fell onto his well-worn and shabby patterned jacket.

The orchestra faded into a live jazz band, headed by a strange-looking man dressed head to toe in bright pink. Jelton Ohn really looked like he was in his element. Seated high up on the wooden roof rafters, he commanded the eye of every person in the room, serenading top hits into the misty night.

"Okay, darlings, this is a little… delicate little number called *Black Beauty,*" he announced, to raucous applause. He burst away into a jaunty tune, and the crowd joined in.

There was much drunk and lots more eaten and the evening was drawing into the early hours. Churchill surveyed the room, his eyes lazily scanning his famous friends. Seated next to Heathen Stawkings, he had zoned out of Stawkings' conversation. He raged on about a candy delivery service to the moon he was working on developing. Candy that could change colour and candy whose taste one could "see" in front of their very eyes.

Snippets of conversation drifted in and out of Churchill's ears.

"All the way and back, on board a shooting star..." Stawking explained delightedly, eyes bulging with excitement to anyone who would listen.

"It would only occur twice a month, and obviously not available in the states... too cloudy," he added quickly, as the nineteenth American President Rutherford twisted his neck around with a furrowed brow.

"Impossible to catch sight of these things across the pond, you need linear, *twinkly* weather... nothing quite like merry England for that."

"Quite right," boomed Churchill, agreeing for the first time with him. "These Americans... hmffff," he puffed as he took another long drag from his cigar.

Elio watched and listened to these strange scenes from the top table. He felt like he was trapped in some old Hollywood film — he still couldn't quite believe he was seated next to these amazing people — people who should all be as dead as dust right now. They all spoke funny. He pinched himself as The Master started:

"You working on anything new, old chap?" Fitzroy directed at Eweton, eager to steer clear of politics. He could see a storm brewing in the thunderous mouth of the ex-prime-minister.

"Yes, quite, as a matter of fact," Newton replied eagerly.

"My apples are coming along nicely, you know. A lot sweeter... and... maximum levitating height 4.69 metres, only recorded last week," he said coyly.

The attention now turned to Eweton, and most were glad not to be on the receiving end of yet another lecture on the 'shortcomings of America' by the ex-Prime Minister.

"I'm branching out to other fruits you see, including the humble berry. The recipes should be blossoming soon. Speaking of which, who's ready for pudding?"

The sweet serenading voice of Jelton subsided to a mere hum and tummies rumbled in deep thoughts of pudding. Up to this point in the night, people hadn't noticed that the large figure of King Henry VIII was noticeably missing. And it had not escaped the interests of many. Guests whispered ranging tales, and Elio and the boys knew not who or what to believe.

"I heard he's allowed a hunt every turn of the century," croaked old Mrs Yardapple.

"Bollocks, Dame Yardapple," challenged the archbishop.

"He broke certain rules, disregarded our natural laws, he clearly deserves punishment," he continued.

"Sorry, but what exactly happened with King Henry?" Elio gingerly interrupted.

And so the old fellows huddled around, basking in the warm glow of the roaring fire and told the tale of how arrogant King Henry had tried to defy the odds and thought he was above everyone else. One night, whilst on a lengthy hunt, he had failed to reach his pedestal in time — the statue of himself that stood just outside his chapel, Kings Chapel, by first light. As a result, the fellows had decided to strip him of his power, as the porters had noticed the missing statue the next morning and gone on a wild goose-chase. There had been quite a hoo-ha.

"You don't want to end up like him, now do you, dear?" Dame Yardapple asked with bulging eyes and drooping jaw, as she got up and left in the direction of the bar. Everything was just slowly sinking in, but Elio still had a million-and-one questions. Who to ask? He was starting to doubt his own mind again.

Stop. Elio commanded his mind.

Did I just do that? Did I just control my own mind? Order it to stop? Damn, the human mind is absolutely incredible. It can lie to itself and make itself believe things. It thinks about itself? Ah, now I'm thinking about it thinking. I need to stop. Elio snapped out of his little reverie, just as the shrivelled figure of Dame Yardapple and a couple of her pals vanished as if eaten by the large gaping doorway.

A momentary silence followed her departure.

Through the skylight, Elio saw a single star wink at him rapidly before disappearing entirely, swallowed up by dense cloud. That's how he felt sometimes, he thought. He hadn't quite adjusted to his own world, flying off to university was a huge step for him. He sometimes rapidly disappeared too.

There were so much to learn and so much living and even more learning to do. Elio remembered how he sometimes escaped to the nearby town with his good friend

Gregory Landcoup — the rare time he got to see him, as Greg was nearly always locked in a lab somewhere in the engineering fortress. He realized just how much he relied on his friends. Though sometimes, he did this alone. It was his silent retreat. His own little escape. He found there was something therapeutic about riding the bus to the edge of town, escaping unnoticed just for a wee while. Here, in *his* other world, he looked and looked. Here, in *his* other world, he looked and looked. He looked at all the different cottages, and they fascinated him. Here, he walked on and on, stopping occasionally to notice the people in their little gingerbread houses. To Elio, they didn't have faces but just lived on and on, simply existing. It's like a little TV screen into another world, he thought. Getting glimpses into a rare lightbox, a fish tank, as he liked to describe his trips, was more interesting than being stuck in the library or the art studio. A stray fox brushed Elio's legs, and suddenly, Elio felt detached from everything around him. Confused, he laughed to himself. He brought himself back to my dining hall-breast. And now in that instant, the Whole World, Time, Stories and Music stopped, as Elio stared into the eyes of the room. He could hear his own breathing in sync with the space around him. He watched the ants on the single blade of broccoli that was discarded on the table between him and the others. Then a shadow crossed everything, and the world continued to turn with yet another token in its merry-go-round system.

A small, shattered shard of happiness. That was what this night was.

He felt an urge to make memories, capture this extraordinary night, but not change as a person, like the whole 'university thing' wanted him to.

"I'm still me," Elio said out loud, but thankfully it was unheard under the great din of the orchestra. He shook out of his trance and looked back at his newfound friends. He received a strange look from Peter. Their eyes locked and he blushed hard. He shook himself out of his trance and looked back at his newfound friends. People come and people go, he thought, but he had a sneaky suspicion that this night would bring the five of them closer than ever.

He had discovered a strange alternative world. A world that had existed even before himself, and who had been meeting under cover of darkness for hundreds of years. Not only that, sure, accidentally discovering another world was one thing, but being granted an important position, a vital link and a real role to play in this other world, was quite another. He needed a break from all this. Elio stood up loudly; scraping his chair back against the stone floor made quite the racket.

"The loo…" he spluttered, to which Fitz pointed him down in the direction of the crypt.

***

Meanwhile, in the crypt below, the golden apple crumble sat in wide trays. Glimmering in the dim candlelight of the dreary crypt, it was ready to be plated up and drowned in thick, creamy Clare custard. Sharp footsteps echoed loudly off the stone walls as Wick and Catson slipped inside.

They had managed to gain entry rather easily, laughing at just how silly the mortals were. Why should we have to live in secrecy? Now, all it would take was just one spray of the developed formula liquid, which was designed to counter the process of turning back into stone, and order would be restored.

"Ready when you are," Catson offered, gesturing at the spray bottle. It glinted green in the firelight, like a large oversized dragonfly.

"The mortal world would soon see change. It would soon be ruled by a new power. On this 700th anniversary, the Fantabs would finally break free from their daily imprisonment!"

"Hear, hear," Wick replied, the devilish grin haunting his face lingered momentarily. Just as the two scientists left to return to the waiting army, Elio slipped into the kitchens unnoticed.

Chapter Six
Singing Saviours

The pale moon with her furrowed brow and twinkling eyes looked down wearily at the scene unfolding on my great chest-court. A white mist clung closely to my cobbled skin as the great menagerie army cantered brazenly into Trinity, unheard by the unassuming rowdy crowd inside. Behind the two leading figures, the horseback cavalry was led by a ghostly white knight, clad in rusty armour. He was impossibly tall and his gaunt face was carved as if from light. This was the legendary Arthor of Gog. King. Tyrant. Prisoner. And now an army general, leading a handsome revolt, his statue taken from the dark storage units of The Fitzwilliam. And now, he was the most trusted general of Wick and Catson. Deep from the green undergrowth, drowsy animals abandoned their snug little holes in my pores and climbed out to watch the action unfold. There were shrill shrieks of laughter, many a 'hip, hip hurrah' and a babble of voices mixed with music escaping from within my heart… The party was roaring like a lively lion.

"You really want to liberate these silly drunks, old chap?" Catson asked.

"Wait and see, old sport, wait and see."

Meanwhile, in the small crypt below, Elio paced the length of the room in brisk strides, fireplace to fireplace that bookended my jaw. The grate let out a hearty laugh and a puff of smoke pushed its way deeper into the room. The frost had crept into the creaks of my very teeth. Elio bolted back up the stairs after excusing himself for the loo. He grabbed Old Benji , telling him everything he had seen earlier in the night. Benji stood next to him, rubbing his thin bony hands together; they began to thaw. He picked up his crystal sherry glass and gripped it tighter, praying for his plan to work. Elio spoke of the bizarre army- he didn't even know if it *was* an army, it could've easily been a larger rather large fancy dress party, led by the two strange characters, everything he relayed to the master at such speed that he was soon out of breath and gulped for air, coughing slightly and receiving a hearty thump on the back. He talked non-stop at full speed, describing and worrying as the expressions on Benji's face changed from grave to worse and finally stopped at a drained 'white-as-a-sheet'.

"Don't be silly, boy, you've just had a nasty shock, your head's in a twist. Now, do let's go back inside and join the others, or you'll miss pudding" Benji managed to utter, in a less than convincing tone. Part of him wanted to believe the boy, but god they're just so excitable at that age, and sure enough he would check a few things and confide in Fitz....

Old Benji left the room, and my door-mouth creaked shut slowly. Frustrated, Elio looked around, wanting to and feeling like *doing something*. Ugh, these adults never do understand. He was fuming now.

And that's when he heard the voice.

It seemed to be coming from a small wooden crate, marked in peeling faded letters.

"Come," it commanded in a slippery tone, barely audible over the racket from the party above. Elio's body went stiff, chilled to bone. The voice did not sound human.

And that's when Elio's eyes locked into hers; an apple. Yes, he was not dreaming now, or even if he was, his eyes were wide open, awake. He went and sat on the floor of my jaw-crypt in Trinity, listening to an *apple*. It had a feminine but plump face, rosy but carved, as if by a child. And the apple was talking to him. Telling him things. Elio slapped himself hard. He couldn't feel a thing. The sharp slap left a buzzing, tingly feeling all over his face, spreading and leaking like melted chocolate into the small of his back. He shivered. The apple spoke about an evil plot. *Cliché*, thought Elio at first, but the uneasy feeling of what he saw earlier jolted him back to the danger he could sense. Apparently, the apple said, there was a plot to thwart the Mere Mortals and give entire rule of both day and night to the Fantabs. He spoke of how he had seen the two weary figures come in and tamper with the pudding, explained something about some formula that they had injected in the apple and all her siblings and family, rambling on about revenge and how tonight the university would be no longer. She raged about how her fellow friends had been sacrificed for the pleasure of pudding for the Fantabs. And then the apple stopped talking, rolled over and fell with a slight thud onto the dusty stone floor. Her words had sunk into Elio's mind, and his instinct told him to believe the silly apple. It was an *apple*, for crying out loud, Elio thought. Yet, it seemed to match the events he had seen earlier. He had a gut feeling there was at least some truth to this bizarre confession.

Elio felt a rush of blood go straight up into his head and his stomach did a somersault. He clambered back out into the great court, gasping for air.

He couldn't do it any more. What had he got himself involved in?

His chest was constricting, and he felt faint. Was this where he buckled? Or should he go on? It was all going way too fast. Everything was happening way too quickly. Elio stood in the cool night air, not knowing how long for. Then he sat down. Right in the middle of the floor. And then he lay back and looked up at the velvet sky. Leaning against the cold stone floor, he realised it all and a shivery tingle went down his spine. Yes, it was a lot to take in, but he could take it in, and he will. There's so much more to this world, than this world. A whole *other world*. It's what we wished for as children, right? But then again, this was Elio's reality. It was all happening. And there was simply no escape. He couldn't just walk away, as much as he wanted to, couldn't make it all stop. He had to go on.

He scrambled back up the stairs to join the others, who he found immersed in song. And they were splendid singers, all part of their college choirs. He felt a pang of otherness wash over him again. He wished he was more musical, but alas, his only talent was getting himself into trouble. Oh, and drawing. He was an excellent artist. But, Elio didn't have a single musical bone in his body and sat stumped as the others belted out popular ballads. He swept the apple to the back of his mind.

"Here, Elio, try giving this a read…" Peter offered him a piece of paper with some song scrawled on. He winked at Elio.

"Just follow the notes, reading music is literally the easiest thing," added Rowena, with a coy smile.

"It's not fair," Elio moaned. "I can't… the letters… they just *won't* stay still. They're all… swimming…"

The others laughed heartily, thumping the table.

"Oh golly, now they slid right off the page."

If you looked hard enough, you could see the vein in Elio's forehead throbbing, signalling the cogs turning wildly in his brain, anxious to come up with a plan. I, very much, could see it. He gave up trying to be a singing saviour and his mind slid back to the plot he had been warned about. He knew he had to act now, his mind racing. Elio thought of the easiest thing to do to avoid pudding being served. He cursed himself for not acting in the crypt below, just toppling the large trays there and then would have stopped all this, if there was any truth to the apple's warning. And then his heart stopped momentarily as he watched the waiters bring in the gleaming plates.

A second went by.

The shockingly eccentric Melley seated next to him at the top table chattered away, bits of food flying out her wide-open mouth. Elio stared into the distance, and then fixed his glassy pale blue eyes on a spot above Churchills left shoulder, anxiously awaiting his cue. He knew what he had to do.

Then, Elio gripped the growing grapefruit he had grabbed from the table tightly in the palm of his hand and felt the cut on his finger burn. With an inaudible sharp cry of pain, he looked down to see he had squeezed hard enough that the blood-red juice had begun to trickle down his forearm. His heart pulsing in his throat, he took careful aim, and in the spur of the moment, pelted the fruit hard across the room.

Meanwhile on the top table, the waiter in his shiny new white jacket unloaded the doomed crumble from his trolley. He carefully balanced two plates on each arm and started to lower them with grace towards the polished table, gleaming in the light, almost blinding him.

And then it hit him.

He didn't know what, or where from, he had only momentarily blinked. And it had happened. Elio's aim had been calculated perfectly. The juicy grapefruit had struck the waiter's left arm, causing him to fling the two dishes forwards in a swooping movement and himself topple to the floor. He couldn't believe what he had just done. He was standing up now. He swallowed hard as the whole hall stood in silence. Every breath was held, every eye watching the arching journey of the gleaming white plate. It turned 180 degrees, reaching its peak in the air and floppily emptied its creamy contents. Ejected, the crumble flopped towards the ground with dizzying speed, landing with a splodge directly on the shining bald head of Prime Minister Churchill. The plate smashed to smithereens on the stone floor with a deafening crash and the room shook with such force. An audible gasp escaped from Rowena's lips:

"Serves that racist right!" she uttered quickly; this was followed by a shriek from a golden eagle. Or Zeera Klaus. Elio couldn't tell the difference anyhow. Churchill's face visibly changed colour to a deep aubergine, and a bellowing roar escaped from the depths of his belly.

"What is the meaning of this?!" he demanded. Seated next to him, Dame Yardapple quivered like a jelly. An odd gurgling sound began to sound from her parted mouth. This was followed by a mighty roar, as if from a Lion just outside the great doorway. At that precise moment, the wooden doors of my swollen lips swung open with a groan. Into the room marched the strangest sight the evening had yet seen. The bizarre menagerie army led by Arthur of Gog; his eyes gleaming red — set with rubies that caught the firelight and were set ablaze. In front of him, the comparably smaller and less-evil-looking figures of Wick and Catson thundered down the hall. This was a sight to take in. The atmosphere of the room immediately dropped. People sat entirely gobsmacked. This was not another party trick, not entertainment. They sensed danger. Eweton stared dumbly with his mouth wide open. Eliza Yammond blinked loudly and repeatedly, fumbling terrifyingly with a copper locket around her small neck. Everyone watched as Catson made his way to the top table, climbed onto it and stood proud, unmoving. They continued to watch, looking at him shake the dust out of his hair, unfold his handkerchief and attempt to read the scrawny writing etched on it. He coughed twice, cleared his throat and began in a loud, haughty voice, addressing the whole room.

"The world of FantaBridge has lived in secrecy and oppression for seven hundred years."

He paused, scanning the room with a squint.

"You great, great, men and women sit by idle and do nothing! Can we really let the mere mortals rule over us when we have inhabited this city for hundreds of years? They pass power from generation to generation when we are infinite and immortal; a constant! Bow down to our new age, and your new rulers," he bellowed loudly.

"I have created something with the elegance and deep simplicity of physics. It will feel almost as if one had been born again. Let us reverse the very structure and core of our world. Do we really need to live our lives on a merry-go-round? watching our time waste away? On the whims of silly children?"

A hush had fallen over the huge hall. There was an air of awesomeness about him as he addressed the room of equally brilliant figures, slowly convincing them of his bid to take over the mortal realm.

"We have the moon, and now we also want the sun. Now, let a new era dawn."

"NO!"

The single voice pierced the air.

The whole room turned to face Elio. His pulse was racing and small beads of sweat appeared on his forehead. He clasped his clammy, sweaty hands together and gingerly rose. This was it now. There was no going back. He revelled in the spotlight, and he summoned every ounce of confidence to say what he was about to say. He had to convince these age-old academic giants his world was worth hiding for. The Mere Mortals simply *had* to rule. It was the only way forward, no new era, but a new generation. There was a split in the room now, and he was certain some were agreeing with Wick and Catson. The only way forward to have a harmonised world, was to let the two worlds co-exist, not have one trample the other. A new era, a new generation, but which side will he then belong to? No, they must keep it like it's always been. Elio fancied himself wise for his nineteen years, yet his skin glowed brightly and turned the same shade of red as a beetroot. He voiced all this in babble, ending loudly with

"DON'T EAT THAT PUDDING! IT'S BEEN POISONED," he shouted to the room, not caring who was listening.

"You're too late, boy, I'm sure pudding is well and truly over," smirked Wick. A grey shadow crossed the room, as people began to realise just what had happened. Catson blew into his blue-spotted cotton handkerchief rudely and banged a clenched fist on the table. The room replied with a stone-cold glare. Bollocks he thought. His world came crashing down around him. He had failed. He was on the brink of glory and this silly little boy had ruined. His eyes watered at the site of the overturned trolley and shattered plate.

Then, without notice, he ran like a madman, tripping over his own feet as he realised his defeat, just as the room erupted in shouts.

"Seize him!" commanded the loud husky voice of Al.

The pudding lay simply abandoned as everyone in the room scrambled towards the two helpless figures. From the middle of the throng, Wicks voice came spiralling out:

"Attack!"

In a moment's flurry, the whole hall charged at each other, the two sides clashing and clanging. Many followed the suit of the young leaders as they charged forward, Rowena tying her long hair back and advancing headfirst into the heat, Christies' leaping over a table. The crowd parted as the muscular figure of Max dived deep and headlong onto Wick, who collapsed in a heap of dusty velvet.

Golden spears arched to the ceiling and landed with thuds into polished wood, pistols were let off, triggers pulled. There were screams of pain, shouts of anguish and bloodcurdling bellows. Following Rowena's lead, the party threw food, using discarded chicken bones to take out enemy eyes. Cutlery clanged around them as the now fragile and broken menagerie army showed signs of retreating. A great deafening din was breaking out now. My mouth had many sores now and I wished I could just snap my jaws shut, tight and crush them all. Have they no respect for my architecture? I let out a shaky groan and my teeth rattled. Everyone suddenly stopped, as the tremor of my mouth shook them out of their battle-reverie. , Eventually the last of the army, who longed to be back in the safe haven of my Fitzwilliam heart retreated. Many deemed themselves too priceless to be destroyed in battle.

The dust settled over my dry mouth as the fighting finished. My mouth was not made for war. Great ulcers now dotted my previously smooth gum. I was angry.

"I'm sure they'll have more value at auction with a couple of broken legs," laughed Peter, as the battle slowly started to subside.

"What?" Elio replied as he locked eyes with Peter. His thighs hurt as they both collapsed onto my tongue-floor. "I feel as though something remarkable has just happened, yet also feel that nothing whatsoever has happened. I feel dazed. I feel like music. Far-away music that tinkles in the distance," Elio continued drowsily. A puff of dust floated down from the ceiling as the last of the headless horsemen cantered out the doorway.

Chapter Seven
Strictly Stone

When a single crow croaks thrice and soars over the Wren Library, whose many window-eyes I use to wink back at it, another night in FantaBridge comes to an end. The fellows of FantaBridge have exactly a dozen and one minutes to get back into position. There is a flurry of activity as everyone rushes to go home. The wind picks up speed and whistles to mask the sound and blur the air. The gargoyles race to the top of the warbled surface of King's Chapel — my adorned breast and Stawkings struggles, heaving his chair back onto his pedestal, the horses canter back into the Fitzwilliam — or Jesus College — if you're the only solitary horse that stands in the middle of Chapel Court, and Eweton clambers back onto the high plinth to resume his stoic pose. All await the magnificent Corpus Clock's banging and clamouring of her many hands. She strikes six with a deafening bang. That signals the end of another day in FantaBridge and each figure starts to weaken. But tonight was no ordinary night. Much of it had been taken up by the peculiar events and now, panicking, the retiring fellows realised with a jolt that they had less than an hour left — they were glad to have an extra hour tonight, if it wasn't for the milky moon annual holiday, they were sure to have been exposed.

The unforgiving wrath of the clock would soon be upon them, and sure enough, minutes later, they heard the faint distant drone of the beast, humming along the quiet streets, her eyes peeled.

Within the cosy warmth of my ageing face, the struggling figures of Wick and Catson lay bound and gagged in the middle of the great hall. They had confessed to everything.

"This is what we'll do, chaps. Gather round — and for goodness sake, pin that brute down!" Al ordered, pointing a wagging finger at the squirming lump of Catson on the cold stone floor. They were aware time was running out; if they didn't decide what to do with the criminals, they won't be able to until the next night. And what if they have some more formula left, and try something again?

"We'll have to pull a 'King Henry' here, folks," Al and Benji addressed the room.

"Hear, hear," shouted Churchill in response and the hall was soon filled with roars of "Bravo!" and "Quite right." The younger fellows watched on, perplexed.

"We'll take them to their respective pedestals," Benji continued, now addressing the group of impish boys lead by Rowena, as they stood heroically, waiting and ready for their first orders

"Sorry, sir, forgive me, but take them back? Surely they will then continue to exist?" enquired Max.

"Ah, dear boy, ever too keen, you are. Let me explain. We take them back... but this is where I find my plan really relishes punishment. You fellows stand guard, and pin 'em down as they try to clamber onto their pedestals.

We show them their chance of escape, right before their eyes, within their reach. We savour watching their pain as they are denied that very freedom that their hands ache to touch. We deny them the same freedom that they were planning to deny the Mere Mortals, whose realm we *borrow* every night. He looked down, repulsed at the two criminals.

"And that ought to teach everyone a lesson, as they slowly but surely turn to stone, their veins drier than bones. The first morning light will hit them with a blow deeper than death. And forever, they stand, carved in stone."

"An excellent plan, we'll play our part well, won't be boys?" Rowena chirped in, nodding at Al and Benji.

"Sir, this may seem like a stupid question…" began Peter. He brushed the hair away from his face and began again.

"Why would it have been so awful for our two realms to mix? Would really have been so bad?"

Every eye turned to him. Elio's eye caught his. For a moment he held it there as everyone weighed the innocence of the question. Many had wondered it but few dared to ask. the secrecy, the hidden nature of the realm they occupied was all part of the tradition. A secret little · club. There were too many of these in Cambridge already. But yet, here was this shy, smirking boy, asking what no one had dared asked before. There was a long pause.

Al stepped forward, right over the two criminals' bodies.

" There are things you don't understand…" he began in a grave tone. "And that's not at all your fault. You are young, modern things. Your world is changing. And fast. There are new ways of life, things one can and cannot say. Technology is developing- and god knows that will wreak havoc with Eweton's wig"-a jolly laugh rippled through the crowd, as Eweton held on ever tighter to his tight curls-laws are changing. "There are so many problems with the past, their attitudes on people's lives- and owning them-, sexuality, religion- all this cannot change all of a sudden for it is their way of life, what they're used to. And we know it's wrong, so why do we still entertain these people? In Fantabridge, the *individual* is NOT celebrated, rather the *work* of that individual is. We cannot educate them further- they are effectively dead. They are a part of where we have come from. They cannot impose their age-old views onto current peoples. They are simply wrong and must remain in the past. The people of the past will never understand the people of the future. We each have our moment in time and to that we are bound. However, occasionally, the dead do not like to be trapped in this space. They want to continue their work. But work ethics have changed. And there simply isn't enough space. We must now give the time to the Ewetons' and Melleys' of today, a chance for *them* to shine and discover and learn. Our two worlds need to remain separate- this wonderful institution lets us borrow time to have a bit of fun here and there, but ultimately, our time is up. You are the future."

An audible sigh of wonder went up in unison. It al made sense now.

Without further ado, the boys and Rowena, finding solace in each other's company as 'the mere mortal outsiders' had bonded surprisingly well and set about doing what they'd been told, wasting no time. And so, the plan was put into action and everyone busied themselves, playing a part. Bodies were lugged and the spoils of war were swept and order was restored. A tottering Seypes was helped onto his pedestal by a struggling Rowena and Max, who both collapsed into a heap after the struggle. It was a strange scene to witness, but racing against time, the fear of being revealed, and with the deadly drone of the Corpus Clock, it was all managed without a hiccup. The new guardians paused for breath. They had done it! Really saved the day — well, night, in this case. and to top it all off, Elio had managed to save pudding. No, not the measly apple crumble, for that was surely ruined, but pudding as a course in this feast to end all feasts. Elio had had the brilliant idea of rustling up crepes as the remaining mass of people demanded pudding. They were a huge hit and a satisfyingly sweet end to such an eventful party. Crepes were the one thing Elio definitely knew how to cook. His Mama had taught him well.

Elio had sprinted down to the kitchens, the others following him. They just about found all the ingredients readily available in Trinity's well-stocked pantry. Memories from Elio's childhood days grazing in the south of France, his mother teaching him her secret recipe that had been perfected for generations was quickly resurrected. With a bolt, he realised he was missing the key ingredient that would make these the most-best, tastiest, satisfyingly, mouth-wateringly delicious crepes ever.

"Christies!" he yelled across the echoey room as Max's broody voice muttered an acknowledgment.

"We need beer- and quick" Elio continued. I know you're the only one who can sneak into to the Eagle & Child and fetch us a barrel…." Elio flashed a smile.

Without a word, the dark-haired figure streaked out the room and returned within minutes with the desired ingredient.

"So, *this* is how the French do it?"

"Oui, oui, my friend, this is why our crepes are silky smooth. A dash of this and I'll have everyone begging for more."

"You'll put the crepe van on Market Square out of business," Rowena added with a hearty laugh.

"Oui, oui, baguette!" chirped Peter, a response he thought French enough in his broken schoolboy accent. Soon, the crepes were piled high on silver platters, dusted with a shower of icing sugar and sent up to be devoured in the hall. It truly was a magical sight to behold. They kept coming, more and more, until everyone had scoffed their faces and the angry shape of the Corpus Clock hissed, hovering by the windows to the hall. The buildings themselves, from the young bricks to the old wide arches, hummed with excitement, as the shadow of King's Chapel loomed over all the different buildings. Slowly but surely, the warm honey-coloured stone started to thaw, and the statues and statuettes turned more and more solid by the minute. The entire operation was managed like clockwork, quite literally presided over by the notoriously nasty and ruthlessly irritating Clock of Corpus. This golden creature took the shape of a six-winged wasp, with horrifying horns on the front of his head. The Corpus Clock buzzed around in the early hours of dawn, ensuring everyone who had roamed the streets during the night was back in their position. She stung and hissed and buzzed and growled till everyone was scared witless, plain-looking as if nothing whatsoever had ever occurred. She had grown tired of her endless searches, but everyone knew and respected her, and she had kept everyone in check for over seven-hundred years. It was a near-miss tonight, but luckily, thanks to Elio, All was fine. As the last of the fellows floated away, The group downstairs hugged and soon sadly dispersed, crazy tired.

"What you need is a stiff drink." Peter had followed Elio down the street. "You look like a startled fish!"

Elio, smirking, shot him a shy glance.

"Goodnight," Peter whispered, ruffling his dark floppy hair. Elio felt a throbbing jolt in his chest that shot down into his navel. His lips went dry and he stuttered a shy, "Night." That stupid feeling, right in the pit of his stomach. God! Why was his mind, heart and body not in sync? He shrugged the thought away.

A small part of him hoped Peter wasn't going to give in easily; and sure enough, when Elio turned for a final look at that tall, slightly lanky tousle-haired boy with spots and a crooked smile, Peter began again.

"That drink…" he muttered, holding out a silver hipflask that shone in the misty morning light.

"Haha, go on then, sleep is for the boring, the weak…" Elio replied. He had a strange suspicion the night was not over yet.

The boys exchanged knowing glances, guiltily smiling and silently headed down to the banks of my blood-red river. They hopped over a small hedge, untied an ageing rope and descended down a set of stone steps set in a aching archway that lead to the edge of the water. Here, they sat drinking away till first light. I flowed on, my current electric and my stream of consciousness unstopping. I felt envious of the two, how their bodies easily shelled together so naturally. My body was extensive and inhabited and weighty. And I didn't have a companion. Let's be honest, I am neither here nor there. Neither alive nor dead. I am city and I'm a town and I'm a home and I'm a house. I simply exist, waiting and watching and telling stories. There they sat drinking away, talking and filling each other up on the eighteen years of life they had lived apart. What a night it had been; the boys' bones numb and aching, waiting till first light. Elio felt as though someone had turned up the brightness of planet earth, he saw everything so crystal clear. He looked up and smiled, and then his eyes fell upon the lithe body of his companion. His midriff was exposed, shining in the pale light. He had fallen asleep on Elio's lap; he shook him awake. Dazed, Peter woke up and as everything fell into place, he realised where he was. His face broke into a huge grin.

The two boys looked at each other and laughed, their faces inches apart, bedazzled, awake, alive and lost, their gazes never faltering, breathing harder and faster, the world went quiet and it was simply just the two of them. The sun was peeking out from behind the horizon line and the first of the early risers were beginning to fumble about their day. Elio noticed the night workers, the construction men, binmen, fixer-uppers and travellers all awake, all going about their daily lives, unknowing. He'd never noticed how vital workers worked to ease life for the rest of us.

Sweating slightly, Elio sauntered back to his room, leaving Peter at Trinity. The creamy clouds parted and the first of the sweet morning dewy light was filtering through the cool clouds. A jaunty step in his walk now, the night had been a whirlwind and too much had happened. His body ached with excitement, a balloon was swelling inside him, knowing that he had been a part of something so profound. A sensitive boy, his eyes became blurry and started to tear up. The whole world as he knew it appeared colourful, with euphoria and happiness pulsing through his veins. He halted, gathering his wits about him.

He had saved an entire people! Everywhere he turned, he couldn't help but beam, hairs raising, a riot of colour dancing in front of him. He skipped through the twisting lanes, hardly believing the events that had unfolded. The dripping of a tap could be heard in the distance as the clock chimed quarter to six. His skin buzzed and tingled, and he found, as he took three stairs at a time and jumped into his warm bed, he couldn't even sleep for grinning ear to ear.

Music was playing in his head and he hummed along, knowing how stupid he sounded but not caring in the slightest.

Elio sat upright on his bed. He laughed for a while, out loud, until his jaw ached. The light streaming through the gaps in his curtains, like a pink sunset cloud, settled on his floor.

He knew it wasn't a dream.

He felt like they were watching him now, now that he was a part of something bigger. How many people had taken this route before him? Who would you ask about all things FantaBridge? And he was sorry that the disappointing answer to all these questions in his head was that he didn't know. There are a lot of things that a lot of people don't know. But there are also a lot of things that Elio did know. It all felt very real, but exhausting. He looked forward to spending yet another night in FantaBridge and felt giddy about how everything was going on under everyone's noses — and no one suspected a thing!

The only boy awake now, watched as ever by the knowing smile of the riot-of-colour portrait of Miss Marylin Monroe that he'd painted himself hung above his mantlepiece. A carol of birds announced daybreak. Elated, Elio Husseini rolled over, fluffed his pillow and was asleep, just as he could've sworn the face of his wall clock winked at him heartily.

The buildings themselves, from the young bricks to the old wide arches hummed with excitement, as the shadow of King's Chapel loomed over all the different buildings. Slowly but surely, the warm honey-coloured stone started to thaw, and the statues and statuettes turned more and more solid by the minute. In truth, I also ,liked a lot of things. I love the feel of little feet pattering about on my skin and the whoosh of cars and bikes and trains and busses as they rumble deep within the recesses of my body from corner to corner. It keeps me alive. It keeps me on my toes. And I learnt to love the little humans. They take care of me so well. One hears of stories of my ancient family far away laying in ruin. The humans have all left. I shudder and a few street lamps flicker. And one very naughty chap-lamp jumps. I remember what it felt like to have someone inside me for the first time. Oi. You. Stop smirking I can see you! The golden creature, I watch, her body in the shape of a six-winged wasp, with horrifying horns on the front of his head. The Corpus Clock buzzed around in the early hours of dawn, ensuring everyone who had roamed the streets during the night was back in their position. He stung and hissed and buzzed and growled till everyone was scared witless, plain-looking as if nothing whatsoever had ever occurred. He had grown tired of his endless searches, but everyone knew and respected him, and he had kept everyone in check for over 400 years. All was fine. He flew, skimming the tops of the city, checking for every nook and cranny. As he zoomed through Tennis Court Lane and took a sharp right at Cherry Tree Close, he halted suddenly, took a sharp intake of breath and narrowed his eyes. He stared hard for a while at the niche that was home to Wick. Empty. The stone was cold, dusty and deserted. This was going to be a stressful morning, a race against time. His anger pulled through his body as the search for the missing began. And then a flashing light signalled him down, down towards Trinity. Waiting there was Old Benji and Dear Al.

"We need to fill you in on many, many bits and pieces, dear Clock…." they began.

"Firstly, you won't be seeing us much longer…"

Chapter Eight
Frisky Fairies

Elio awoke the next day, not fancying heading to his lectures. You couldn't blame him, surely? After the night he had had. He deserved a month off. His alarm had gone off at 8:50 a.m., and he'd ignored it, and later awoke realising there was no way he was going to get dressed and cycle halfway across town just to listen to yet another ageing male talk about bricks. Last night had been educational enough. He had interacted with architecture, convincing himself he was at work until the early hours. He laughed at his own silly cleverness, and decided to have a lengthy lie-in. Dangerous, but all in the name of self-care. His mental-health was important after all and he needed his beauty sleep.

An hour later, or what felt like an hour but was probably three, Elio shot up when a jolt of pain shuddered up his spine. Glancing at the wall clock, he realised he had slept into the early hours of the afternoon. He had strained his back pretty hard, running, jumping and climbing. It'll get better it's only a little pain, he thought, pushing it to the back of his mind. He later realised this was a huge mistake.

Elio got up and absent-mindedly threw something on and sauntered out onto the bright sunlit court, his eyes hurt, and his body ached. A fine layer of powdery sunshine had blanketed itself cosily over my whole body, Elio barely recognising where he was going as the buildings shape-shifted undercover of this magic light. He trudged along the well-beaten path until he turned a corner and the familiar sight of Trinity greeted him.

"Elio!," someone shouted across the lawn. He could just about make out a small pale figure waving frantically at him. He squinted his eyes.

Why, it was Kitty!

Kitty Celeste had a shock of spiky blonde hair that was stiff as rock cakes to touch and glinted in the weak morning sun. She bobbed towards Elio in a floaty floral winter dress, her voice shrill, waving madly. Elio could've sworn he saw a pair of glittery wings jitter behind her. She was so fairy-like, and he wouldn't be surprised if she sneezed a bag full of golden fairy-dust.

"Prang!" she stumbled loudly, stopping next to him, out of breath. Elio nodded and flashed a toothy smile. He was just about to go into overdrive, spilling everything from last night when he stopped short. He wasn't *meant* to say *anything* to any other student. He had taken a solemn oath.

"How're you, my bagel?" she proclaimed loudly.

"ANGEL. I meant *angel*." She guffawed, her front teeth twinkling, both of them unable to control their laughter.

"Sorry, my daft head was floating off again."

Bursting to say at least something, he suggested they head down to the river with a picnic. He was starving. The feast had ended nine hours ago and his tummy rumbled audibly.

"What a jolly brilliant plan," Kitty said, her eyes lighting up and boiling over with ideas of what to bring.

"I'll just nip into my room to grab my fluffy blanket. It tastes so good. " And she sped off. Elio stood there, dazed. She was back within a heartbeat and they sauntered arm in arm across the dying, yellowing grass, down towards the banks of the River Cam. They sat there for what felt like forever, watching and laughing at all the punts laden with tourists went by. And then, one of the punts veered towards them and a girl was waving her hand high, shouting his name.

"Hullo Elio!" She flashed a wide smile. A pretty, tanned girl rowed up to them, and the punt bumped against the bank, sending water sloshing into the gardens.

"Fancy seeing you here?!C'mon, mate, jump in!". She brushed her long brunette hair away from her face and wiped her sweaty brow. Her emerald green shirtdress was unbuttoned and had just fallen off her left shoulder. She stood, beaming.

Maliya Giovanni looked simply radiant. She was good-natured, but stubborn and strong-willed. Elio had gotten to know her rather well, both in and out of lectures. They'd often skip off work to hang out and Maliya would summon the most fantastic feasts to bring along on their little excursions. Elio, with kitty at his heels, walked over to the edge of the river. He took a jaunty step and shook the narrow, flat vessel as he climbed on.

"Kitty, you too, hop on!" Maliya encouraged.

She jumped up on her tiny feet and edged towards the water. Here, she gave a little wobble, and at that precise moment, Elio slumped down on the thin plank of wood.

And down went Kitty. The boat shook and with a sizable splash, Kitty-Celeste was smack bang in the depths of the River Cam. The look on her face was simply priceless. There was no high-pitched scream. Just utter shock. And then came the laughter; Maliya and Elio laughed so hard that Kitty, with her now flattened spikes, was forced to crack a smile, gushing about in the water and slowly heaving herself onto the punt. She sat there, like a balloon which had just lost all its air, dripping wet. Another ridiculous bout of laughter followed as the party drifted off downstream, the sun baking Maliya's olive skin golden; she constantly complained about it.; while Kitty thanked its presence in hopes it may restore her to her original state. They were nearing Elio's college, and he stopped them short, suddenly.

"Drop me off here will you, gals? I've got to shoot off." Elio looked at the ground guiltily, thinking of where he was heading. He blushed. The girls took the hint and teased him until he was forced to run, their taunts ringing in his ears. He stood waiting at the Porters Lodge when a familiar tall figure appeared from the Queens Road bend.

I'll show you around my college if you fancy," he had muttered yesterday morning to Peter. Classic Cambridge excuse to see someone again, thought Elio, sheepishly. And after the tumultuous time they'd spent bonding over beastly plans, Peter had agreed.

"Hey, Peter." Elio started, motioning up and around him. "Welcome to my humble abode," he sniggered.

"June," Peter responded curtly after he'd said hi and how ok he was.

"What?" Elio stared at him blankly, thinking he had completely misread the entire scenario, his ears turned red. Had he gotten things wrong?

Peter stared right back and repeated, "June."

A low panic started rising in Elio's belly. Was this the same boy from twenty-four hours ago?

"It's what they call me, you know."

"Who's they?" Elio spluttered.

"Those who know me better than they think. And those who mean something to me," he offered, matter-of-factly.

"Right."

"It's just, you shouted 'Hey, Peter,' across the courtyard…"

Elio's face broke into a coy smile.

"June…" Elio whispered back. "It's beautiful. But why?"

"It's coz my birthday's in June, silly" He chortled.

The two boys set off, wandering around fairly pointlessly, content to be in each other's company, knowing the other shared their own heavy burdens and duties.

And then it slapped him in the face as to why he was here with his new friend.

"Of course, the architecture!" Elio almost shouted.

He was all excited now, his pulse quickening. He began to explain, much to June's delight, the buildings that he called home. Yes, Elio, this boy of eighteen talked wonderfully about my body. It's history. Its quirks. And I almost puffed out in important happiness. June watched with a curious smile while Elio rambled on, pointing high above and bending down below, highlighting this and outlining that, until he'd painted a full picture of the illustrious history of the college and how it had been shaped by architecture. How it was continuing to be shaped by it.

"See, it's the one phenomenon mankind cannot escape, June" Elio shouted, walking backwards so he could face his one-man-tour. He sped up, leading June into the narrow stone archway that turned right into the chapel.

"Where there are humans, there is architecture. We go hand-in-hand." Elio finished, almost breathless.

"You're getting the hang of it! you called me June…"

"Shut up, you." They broke into laughter.

They found themselves in an intimate barrel-vaulted space, with golden octagons carved into the roof. Yellow sunlight was streaming into the room through the tall stained-glass windows. Dark wood carved the pews that faced each other, leading the eye up to the magnificent painted altarpiece.

"Ethereal, isn't it?" Elio asked.

"Beautiful and oddly welcoming though," June responded. This was probably because it was empty, he thought. He had plenty of experience in chapels, dragging himself for the long choir rehearsals, endless concerts and prayer services he had to present. Elio, on the other hand, didn't see the chapel for what it was; a Christian space. He only saw the lines and angles and corners and windows and materials that made up the space. Space. It was all architectural.

They walked down the uneven tiled floor. Where the sunlight hit it, the dazzling black and white tiled floor appeared as a mirage. Sat on the cold wood and enjoying the warmth, Elio could've sworn the wings of the androgynous angel fluttered slightly. This was *not* happening again. It's not night time yet.

"I think I saw the virgin's blue robe slide off her knee," June said out loud, perplexed.

The boys knew they were bound to each other through this one burden. A secret they must live to protect.

"I thought all the interesting stuff happened at night." Elio smiled, internally carefully yet outwardly casually placing a hand on June's tightly wrapped denim thigh.

June flinched and then relaxed his tense body.

"I guess this stuff happens during the day sometimes... or the suns playing tricks on us."

Elio picked up an ageing, tattered leather-bound Book of Common Prayer, small enough to sit comfortably in the palm of his hand. June said something about how he used to visit his grandmother in rural Wessex, and how he was looking forward to making more music with his electric guitar, but Elio wasn't paying too much attention. He flicked through the rotting pages and absent-mindedly started to ink in the scene in front of him. An architect never went anywhere without a pen.

"You drawing me?" June enquired gleefully.

"No, just the building, ya know." Elio smirked back.

"Ah, I thought I was an actual muse there for a split second... I'll just go cry my eyes out..."

"God's an architect; you know that," Elio spluttered suddenly.

"How?" June looked sceptical. "Please expand Boyo..."

"Well, the creationist argument" Elio started, before he was rapidly cut off by June

"You're just saying that to make yourself feel better and were sitting in a chapel"

"No, believe me. Everything in this entire universe has been designed so perfectly.

June nodded.

"There are so many intricate systems, working in place, harmoniously. Look at the water cycle... heck, look at your body... Elio smiled, placing his hand flat on Peter's chest. Their eyes locked.

"I know, it's perfect," Peter smirked.

" Hundreds of systems, working together to make you the best version of you, all enclosed in a beautiful shell. So perfect. It can't have happened by accident. It must have been designed."

June looked back, not entirely convinced but seemingly welcoming.

"Yes, he sat down with a piece of paper, sketched out an idea and then made a model and then made the real thing- The Ultimate Architect."

"Interesting theory, mate. Ever thought of getting a personality that stretches beyond your degree?"

And then, loudly, "HOLY MOLY is that a Bible?"

"No, just a glorified history textbook," Elio replied.

"What're you doing, drawing in it? That's blasphemy!"

"Adding to history," Elio whispered enchantingly, with a glint in his eye.

"And besides, I thought you didn't care much for religion? Elio continued nonchalantly, aware of the glow he had about his face. he was feeling very hot. But he was sure and most confident in himself.

There was a pause, as June registered everything Elio had just said. It was a lot to take in.

"I could kiss you," June said, exasperated, looking in absolute awe at Elio.

What happened next, both boys hoped the mirage-like sunlight had blinded the cameras too...

***

Elio retreated back to his room and lay spread-eagled on his bed, thinking over the events of the last few days. Bored, tired and hungry, he escaped into the corners of his mind in the hope of entertaining himself. All his friends were busy working. He just didn't feel like it.

He lay there, thinking. I could see how his mind was working. Running away with itself. Was he anything special? He started to confide in me; thinking out loud. No, not really, he disagreed with himself. This ever-changing world that he lived in, was it really properly changing? Or was it just repeating itself like a broken record? I was the constant. On that we agreed. To him, greatness had already been achieved. Was he merely a pawn but playing his own beautiful role. Yes, there really was something out there too... Elio savoured the moment, enjoying getting lost in the liminal, parallel space that was his imagination. In the grand scheme of things, he was just Elio. Elio Husseini, a boy with a plan, with a heart and head to match and rival each other.

Elio sauntered down the flat stone steps and darted straight for the tall wooden doors to the great hall. Another night had ended, and he could not wait to have another adventure In Fantabridge. He had last visited it almost a week ago, and simply hadn't had time to go again. There was no denying just how demanding his studies were becoming. He found himself drawing, experimenting, creating and writing away for hours on end. He found solace in doing all this with his friends and colleagues. That was the one thing he loved about being in this place. In Cambridge, he was never far away from a cup of tea with someone. He could waltz into his friends' rooms in less than a minute, when he was too bored of his own company or had worked his absolute hardest and needed a break. It really wasn't anything like his house.

Dodging some drunken darlings on their way to each other's beds, Elio had made it to the foyer outside the hall.

At the double doors, his body made an immediate left turn and inched toward the smaller door concealed perfectly flush against the carved panelling. He pushed carefully, and to his delight, it swung open, revealing a smaller room than expected. It was pretty much just a broom cupboard. Inside, a single stuffed armchair, a thin rickety table with a marble top and an absolutely humongous painting of a rather dashing young man. The man's profile was painted with such delicate strokes, you could almost touch his petal-soft skin. He had a peach complexion that complimented the heavy gilded frame that trapped him.

Elio took a seat. He sank deep into the depths of the chair, as it almost swallowed him.

As soon as he sat down, the figure changed. Looking up at him from this angle made him appear gaunt, with swollen eyes as big as tennis balls. Elio sat there, waiting for something to happen.

Nothing did.

Not until Elio brought his sketchbook out and started drawing the figure did it speak.

Elio jumped with shock as the man started:

"Hello, Elio."

Elio just started back at him. Suddenly the room was too small for the both of them. And then the figure stepped casually out of his frame, jostling it a little as he teetered onto the floor.

The sharp painting of a man explained that he was the former Won Bankes — MP for Cambridge University many moons ago when it used to be its own constituency, and a fellow trinitarian. He explained that Elio's drawing of him had stirred something within the painting he was trapped in, the two inks' had connected. And that he was determined to make a new friend today. He told him all about his extensive travels to the middle east and all his exciting discoveries.

"Why're you shoved away in this tiny room if you've done so much with your life?" Elio demanded.

"Well, back in '41, Eighteen, that is, there was a bit of a run-in with the law. We won't go into too much detail here my dear boy, there is much work to be done," Bankes replied sheepishly.

"Who am I to judge someone's past, right — it's all about how you are with me right now in this very minute. And I find you perfectly savoury. Let's keep it that way, shall we?" said Elio

"Well, I've got to go on a lil' pilgrimage tonight, would you care to join?"

Bankes' told Elio how he had to travel to Ely tonight...

How he simply had to find out the origins of day, to see where the sun rose from, where architecture came from and Ely was the place that held all the answers to these age-old secrets. And so, Elio was snatched from his cosy home in honeyed Cambridge, flying, pedalling the wind to transport him miles and miles away. in the impressive shadow of a gothic masterpiece; Ely Cathedral, he stood erect. And what he discovered inside this building changed his life and his mind forever.

"Life is but a game of dressing up" Elio Husseini said out loud to no one in particular.

Ninety-seven years later

The cast bronze opened one eye. He surveyed the inside of my slender arms. I was almost holding him, protecting him as if he were my own. Elio Husseini's new chambers cradled in my palm suited the world-explorer, discoverer-of-a-new-nation, toy-maker and former master of the new college the Mere Mortals had created — D'Hassan College Cambridge. Elio wished he had a full body but the sculptor had only created his face. Students now rubbed his nose for good luck before they entered the examination schools. It tickled. A lot had changed in the architecture of my body. For starters, there was a new faculty — built on the moon. The husseini Faculty for space exploration was now an exclusive centre for astronomical studies. Most Cambridge students could apply to do a year there much like a languages student would do a year abroad. Such a nice break away. I was very envious and often wondered what that beautiful creature, the moon, was really like. She sometimes winked at me when I ejected a Rocket-finger, tucked with students, up to her. What's, more, my body now played host to organised time travel in supervised groups of three. It was all made possible by the specialist new Department of Time Studies and the fellows of Fantabridge had actually allowed The Corpus Clock to actually lecture the students! I guess there was a breaking down of otherness and barriers between the two realms inside me. Wick and Catson had certainly started a movement... Moreover, Fantabridge now had sister cities that also played hosts to magical realms, twinned with places that had ancient universities such as fez and Bologna. They sometimes sent items such as paintings back and forth. Or even an old brick-tooth of mine. Bits of me inside a whole new person! Speaking of fez, the revolting nightclub of the same name had been demolished and replaced by the new centre for antigravity. This was a shiny new organ I'd gained in which the laws of physics were left at my door. And I tell you, having a drink or three was quite another story in there. Though, I must admit, the coolest bar is the one found at the roof of Kings chapel, on my very face. The infinity pool, made up of my very tears allowed you to swim to the bar. One got very wet in the queue. They had installed this at the same time the chapel was converted to a boutique spa featuring an escape room and a club room in the crypt. This was increasingly popular when work stress got too much for students. They were each allowed to enter my face once a month. And finally, the annual boat race now took place-on borrowed blood of mine they transported down to London-backwards. The rowers faced Richmond while they rowed toward Westminster. And before you ask, yes Maliya did represent Cambridge. But only when she was in her final year and that's the year they chose to switch to backward rowing, so sadly the women's boat lost to Ox***d. In other news, one of my organs stopped working a few years back. They decided to decommission it by bulldozing over it. It was called Robinson and it was blood read and full of the building blocks of life. It's now been replaced with a green stables that features a bee community farm on its roof — Cambridge honey is award winning and second best in Britain. The stables are for the horses that my body became infected with. After the founding horse had a love affair with three ponies living towards my feet, he fathered many, many children. These replaced the Cambridge bicycle and now students cantered everywhere, even when coming back from nights out.

Anyhow, back to Elio. His head now floated toward my heart as yet another night in FantaBridge casually commenced. He stared blankly at his yellowing ceiling. I could hear him go on, faster and faster. It was slightly disconcerting watching him. He wasn't like this the night before. I suppose one night really can change things about who you are. His mind was racing now. I remembered it as if it was only yesterday. He wondered out loud. I'm too much. No, I'm too little. But I'm content with that, I've lived my past life fully without than searching too hard for something good. Because, then, it never comes. But then again, he was just a small cog in a very big well-oiled machine. *They'd* been doing it for hundreds of years, right? And they'd granted him privileged access into a whole new world. He'd have been stupid not to take it, he assured himself. Elio was cementing his place, proving himself to himself firstly. It was silly to say there was a fork in the road.

No.

There was only, simply *one* lonely winding road.

And Elio was going to take it at full speed.

THE END

Acknowledgements

Being published at twenty feels absolutely amazing but was certainly no easy feat. It could never have happened without the love and support of certain people. It's been a long road, and holding my hand all the way and believing in my dreams—*our dreams*—is my dearest sister Maria-'Barj'. I'd like to thank my incredible friends and family, namely Elias Michaut, who helped inspire this, Ryan Wilson, Alex Mitchell, Mila Giovacchini, Lizzy Hammond, K-Lapped and Louis Jackson, and others (you know exactly who I mean) who have characters based on them. Also, everyone at Pegasus, who truly made it happen, and Cambridge University for being my wildest experience. Last but not least, to you, my reader, for sharing this experience with me. Keep on being adventurous and curious about world around you, and maybe, just maybe, one day it will all make sense to you.

Love,
Abdullah